THE COMPLAISANT LOVER

THE
COMPLAISANT
LOVER

A Comedy

GRAHAM GREENE

NEW YORK : THE VIKING PRESS

The Complaisant Lover was first presented on the New York stage on November 1, 1961, at the Ethel Barrymore Theater. It was produced by Irene Mayer Selznick and directed by Glen Byam Shaw, with scenery and costumes by Motley, and had the following cast:

VICTOR RHODES	Sir Michael Redgrave
WILLIAM HOWARD	George Turner
CLIVE ROOT	Richard Johnson
ANN HOWARD	Sandy Dennis
MARGARET HOWARD	Christine Thomas
MARY RHODES	Googie Withers
ROBIN RHODES	Nicholas Hammond
HOTEL VALET	Gene Wilder
DR. VAN DROOG	Bert Nelson

THE COMPLAISANT LOVER

CHARACTERS
(in order of appearance)

VICTOR RHODES
WILLIAM HOWARD
CLIVE ROOT
ANN HOWARD
MARGARET HOWARD
MARY RHODES
ROBIN RHODES
HOTEL VALET
DR. VAN DROOG

SCENES

ACT ONE

SCENE I: A cutlet with the Rhodeses.
SCENE II: Amsterdam: the end of a holiday.

ACT TWO

SCENE I: Home again with the Rhodeses. Nine days later.
SCENE II: The same, after an interval of a few hours.

Act

One

The living room of a house in North London. It is designed to serve as both dining room and drawing room, the walls slanting in the centre towards the footlights and back again, so as to form an inner room rather than an alcove, where the men in the party now in progress are sitting over the wine. There is a sideboard and upstage from the sideboard a door. The men are in dinner jackets.

At the back of the living room tall windows open on to a small garden, but the curtains are drawn. A door opposite the dining room leads to the hall and stairs.

The host, Victor Rhodes, is a man in his middle forties. He has a plump round face, now a little flushed with wine, an air of happiness and good nature. Throughout the scene we are a little haunted by the thought that we have encountered him somewhere before; his anecdotes, of which he has so many, have surely at one time fallen into our own ears. He is on his feet half-way between sideboard and table.

On the right of his empty chair sits William Howard, a local bank manager, a man in his late fifties. The third man, the youngest there, is in his late thirties, with sullen good looks and an air of being intellectually a little more interesting than his companions. He runs, as we soon learn, a local antiquarian bookshop: his name is Clive Root; but the profession of Victor Rhodes—and it is perhaps a professional air which we are trying to identify—remains unknown until later in the scene.

3

The women are upstairs, but they will soon drift down to the drawing room. There is Mrs. Howard, a woman in her early fifties, quiet and kindly; her daughter Ann, a girl of nineteen, pretty and immature, and Mary Rhodes, a woman in the middle thirties, who moves quickly, nervously, with unconscious beauty.

When the curtain rises only the men are there. From the attitude of the men Victor is obviously concluding a long address.

VICTOR: Off on the wrong foot, arse over tip, and there I was looking up at the stars—I mean Oxford Circus. And what did my wife say—"That word in nine letters was escalator." Ha, ha, ha. If there's one thing I thank God for, Mr. Root, it's a sense of humour. I've attained a certain position in life. There are not many men in my profession I would acknowledge as my masters, but I would sacrifice all that—this house and garden, that chair you are sitting on, Mr. Root—it cost me no mean figure at Christie's, I like beautiful things around me— what was I saying, William?

HOWARD: You were telling Mr. Root and me about your sense of humour.

VICTOR: That's right. A sense of humour is more important than a balance at the bank—whatever William may say.

HOWARD: I don't say anything, Victor, you never let me.

VICTOR: Ah-ha, William has a sense of humour too, you see. Perhaps it's not so important in a bank manager as in a man of my profession, but it's not our professions that I have in mind. Mr. Root, you are looking tonight at a very rare phenomenon—two men who are happily married. And why are we happily married?

HOWARD: Because we happen to like our wives.

VICTOR: That's not enough. It's because we've got a sense of humour. A sense of humour means a happy marriage.

CLIVE: Is it as simple as that, Mr. Rhodes?

VICTOR: I can assure you there are very few situations in life that a joke won't ease.

HOWARD: You were going to let us have some port, Victor.

VICTOR: Port? (*He looks at the decanter.*) Oh yes. (*He sits down.*) You, William?

HOWARD: Thanks. You, Mr. Root?

CLIVE: Thanks.

VICTOR: Do you know how this business of passing the port clockwise originated?

HOWARD: Yes, Victor. I learnt it from you. Last week.

VICTOR (*unabashed*): Ha, ha, that's good. I'll remember that to tell my victims.

HOWARD: How are the second-hand books, Root?

VICTOR: You ought to call them antiquarian, William. It's more expensive. Do you know the first thing Dr. Fuchs found in the Antarctic?

HOWARD (*wearily*): No, Victor.

VICTOR: A second-hand Penguin.

He looks from one to the other, but nobody laughs.

CLIVE: The second-hand books would gather a lot more dust, Mr. Howard, if it wasn't for your daughter.

HOWARD: I never thought of Ann as a great reader.

Ann has come down first of the women. She stands a moment as though listening and then picks up a magazine.

5

CLIVE: Her interests are specialized. The early Western. We are talking of you, Ann.

ANN: Only Zane Greys.

VICTOR: Not highbrow, anyway. She's too pretty, William, to be highbrow.

CLIVE (*who obviously has some hidden antipathy to Rhodes*): Brows are a matter of opinion, Mr. Rhodes. The early Zane Greys cost quite a lot already and they are a good investment.

VICTOR: Investment? That's an idea. A man says to me—they often do if I give them the chance—"I'm buying tobacco now for a rise. What do you say?" And now of course I'll tell him "Put your money into Zane Greys."

CLIVE: You'd be giving perfectly good advice. Unless someone discovers that books are a cause of cancer.

HOWARD: At the bank I tell my customers, "Hold on to gold."

VICTOR: Send the port round again, Root.

Mrs. Howard has come down, closely followed by Mary Rhodes.

MARY: She *will* bring in the coffee before I ring. I suppose it's nearly cold.

MRS. HOWARD (*feeling the pot*): Oh, no.

MARY (*with her eyes on the other part of the room*): I wish you'd pour out.

MRS. HOWARD: Of course I will. Sugar?

MARY: Please.

ANN: Oh, Mother—not in mine.

MRS. HOWARD: I forgot she's on a diet. Look up what time the Larkins are on, dear. Your father won't want to miss them.

(*Handing Mary her cup.*) Thank God I'm past dieting. I've got my man.

MARY: We both have, haven't we? (*She takes her cup and goes to watch the men.*)

Her husband has at last found his chance. Clive looks up and sees her. They watch each other while Victor talks.

VICTOR: Now take that chap Farquhar I told you about last week.

MARY (*to Mrs. Howard*): We have them for better, for worse.

HOWARD: Why should we, Victor?

VICTOR (*quite unthrown*): Take him anyway. Most interesting man. He's put his little all into potatoes. He was telling me yesterday that they're growing a new kind which will be pale mauve in colour.

HOWARD: Why?

VICTOR: The ladies will like it. Pretty on the plate. It's the same with oranges. A man in the fruit trade told me you can't sell a green orange. Tastes just the same, but you can't sell them. In South Africa they pass them through gas chambers to make them orange.

MRS. HOWARD: Really!

HOWARD (*trying to switch him*): Could I have a last glass of port, Victor?

VICTOR: Of course, William. Not me though. You, Mr. Root? You have strong young teeth.

CLIVE: What have teeth got to do with it?

VICTOR: Too much wine causes acidity. Acidity causes tartar. Tartar . . .

Mary turns away and goes back to Mrs. Howard.

CLIVE: I'll have another glass. There are worse things than tartar.

VICTOR: Such as . . . ?

CLIVE: The worms that eat my stock. They're like some people, Mr. Rhodes. You can only tell where they have been by the holes they leave behind.

VICTOR: I'm rather a specialist in holes myself.

CLIVE: I thought perhaps you were.

VICTOR: Here's a riddle for you. What kind of thing is it we prefer with holes in it?

HOWARD: Gruyère.

VICTOR: You're the first person to guess.

HOWARD: You told it to me, Victor, a month ago.

VICTOR: It comes of knowing so many people. One forgets to whom one has told what. Believe me, I've told a man his own life history before now.

HOWARD: We believe you.

VICTOR: For goodness' sake, Root. Your cigar. It's burning the cloth.

Clive snatches up a cigar butt and finds it to be only a trick one, the glowing end formed of red paper.

CLIVE: I'm so sorry. Mrs. Rhodes . . .

HOWARD: It's only a fake. Never mind, Root.

VICTOR: You should have seen his face.

MARY: You have to pass an initiation ceremony in this house.

CLIVE: I used to be very fond of these tricks—when I was a child.

VICTOR: You aren't offended, old chap, are you?

CLIVE: No. Interested, that's all. Jokes like this must be a compensation for something. When we are children we're powerless, and these jokes make us feel superior to our dictators. But now we're grown up, there are no dictators—except employers, I suppose.

HOWARD: I'm the only one here who has an employer—if you can call Head Office that.

VICTOR: I just think jokes like that are funny. I don't see why you have to analyse everything.

CLIVE: You should read Freud on the nature of a joke.

VICTOR: Oh, I suppose he sees sex in it. Sex everywhere. (*He holds up the cigar butt vertically.*) Can you see any sex in that, William?

HOWARD: Well, frankly, Victor, yes, I can.

Victor looks at the cigar butt and drops it hastily.

VICTOR: It's time we joined the ladies. Anybody want to wash? The plants can do with a shower. No?

They move into the other section of the room.
Mary watches Clive come in, and so does Ann. Clive's eyes are on Mary.

MRS. HOWARD: If you'd stayed tippling much longer you'd have been late for the Larkins.

HOWARD: My wife always pretends it's I who must see them.

MARY (*to Clive*): Was the port all right? I went to the Army and Navy for it myself.

CLIVE: It was very good, and the cigar butt was very good too. Did that come from the Army and Navy?

MARY: Oh, he has a lot of little tricks like that. He's very fond of bleeding fingers and flies on lumps of sugar.

9

Mrs. Howard is pouring coffee again and Victor is carrying round cups.

VICTOR: Sugar, Mr. Root?

CLIVE: No thanks. (*Mary raises her eyebrows and Clive shakes his head. Victor has passed on.*) He would hardly try to catch me twice in one evening. It would be a bit conspicuous.

VICTOR: Why are we all standing around, William? Here, Root, you'll find this chair comfortable. (*As Clive goes towards the chair, Mary gets there first and, lifting the cushion, removes a small flat cushion.*) Mary, what a spoil sport you are.

MARY (*to Clive*): This plays "Auld Lang Syne." If Victor had disliked you, he has another that cries like a baby and says Mama.

VICTOR: My wife doesn't approve of my jokes, Root, but I have the support of my children.

CLIVE: How old are your children?

VICTOR: Sally's fifteen—she's away at school—and Robin's twelve. At the moment he's passionately in love with Ann here. He'll be down in a minute. It's only the tele that could have kept him away so long.

HOWARD: Has he proposed yet, Ann?

ANN: No. Unless you count giving me a stuffed mouse. He's stuffed it himself—very badly.

HOWARD: He's scientific, is he, like his father?

VICTOR: Oh, Robin and I understand each other. We speak the same language.

MARY: Give him a smile, Ann, when he comes in. The mouse meant a lot. I can never understand why people laugh at children's love. Love's painful at any age.

VICTOR: Oh, come, Mary. I don't find it painful.

Mary turns abruptly away and becomes aware of the way in which Ann is watching Clive. She looks quickly back at Clive, but Clive is unaware of Ann.

MRS. HOWARD: Don't forget the Larkins.

VICTOR: There's time for more coffee first. You can trust me. I've never missed the Larkins yet. Do you know Lord Binlow? He likes them too.

HOWARD: The old Liberal? Is he a friend of yours?

VICTOR: Oh, he comes in regularly every three months. An affable old thing. I have to gag him or we'd never get our business done. He told me the Prime Minister can't understand the jokes. They're too quick for him—like the Russians.

Robin Rhodes comes in in a dressing gown.

ROBIN: Father, only three minutes for the show.

VICTOR: Manners, Robin, manners. Don't you see who's here?

Robin looks across at Ann.

ROBIN: Oh, yes, I do. (*Ann works up a smile for him which immediately raises his spirits.*) Good evening, Mrs. Howard, Mr. Howard. Good evening, Mr. —

MARY: This is Mr. Root, Robin. He has the bookshop near the heath.

VICTOR: The root of all evil. (*He looks hopefully round, but no one laughs except Robin.*)

ROBIN: That's frightfully good. (*He realizes no one else has laughed.*) Isn't it?

HOWARD: Your father has a great sense of humour.

ANN: Have you been stuffing any more mice, Robin?

ROBIN: Oh, no, I only did the one. I shan't do any more. It's not very well stuffed, I'm afraid.

ANN: It was sweet of you to give me your only one.

ROBIN: I'm afraid it's a bit ragged. It'll fall to pieces pretty soon, but then just throw it away.

ANN: I'll keep it in memory.

ROBIN: You could keep an ear, perhaps. That would be quite clean and it wouldn't take up any room. Come on, it's time for the Larkins.

CLIVE (*catching Mary's eye*): I'm like the Prime Minister. I think I'll stay behind with the coffee.

Mary is about to speak when Ann speaks first.

ANN: I'll keep you company, Clive. I don't want to see it either.

Mary hesitates, then leads the way out.

VICTOR (*to Howard as he goes*): We stow the tele away in the old nursery. Mary can't bear that eye watching her. Guilty conscience, you know.

MRS. HOWARD (*as she goes*): I wish we had a spare room for ours, but there's only the cellar.

HOWARD: Can't use that. Door opening and shutting all the time. Upset the wine.

They have all gone.

ANN: Would you like some more coffee, Clive?

CLIVE (*looking at the books on the shelf*): No, thanks. It'll keep me awake.

ANN: Are you a bad sleeper?

CLIVE: Sometimes.

ANN: I can let you have some awfully good pills.

CLIVE: Surely you don't take pills. At your age.

ANN: How I hate that phrase.

CLIVE: What phrase?

ANN: "At your age." They say "Do you still read Westerns at your age?" As though nineteen was middle-aged, and then when I have a Benzedrine at breakfast—

CLIVE: Benzedrine!

ANN: There you are. "Benzedrine at your age," you were going to say, and this time nineteen means something in the nursery.

CLIVE: Why do you take Benzedrine?

ANN: I'm dieting. To get rid of this and this. They call it puppy-fat. Sometimes I want to scream at them—nineteen is a woman. I could have had a child of six by now.

CLIVE: Six?

ANN: Yes, six. I'm one of the early ones. I'm not a puppy, Clive.

CLIVE (*at the shelves*): Why do you read Zane Grey?

ANN: Because England's so damnably small. I can't walk to your shop without seeing four people I know. We all sit around and eye each other like suspects in a detective story. Is Zane Grey less worth reading than Agatha Christie?

CLIVE: No.

ANN: Sometimes I think I'd marry anyone who wanted to get away. Not necessarily marry either. I'm such a bitch, Clive, I have to make an effort even to smile at that little brat with his dried mouse.

CLIVE: Robin's not a bad child, is he?

ANN: They think it funny and rather charming that he's in love with me—and rather a compliment to me. It's all very whimsical because we are both children and we don't know what love really is.

CLIVE: Do you?

ANN: Yes.

CLIVE: Poor you.

ANN: You sound as if you don't much like it either.

CLIVE: No, I don't.

ANN: Clive, let's go away together.

CLIVE: Go away?

ANN: For a time. It needn't be always if you don't like me. It could be a trial week.

CLIVE: Ann, dear, you aren't in love with me.

ANN: How do you know? (*Clive makes a gesture.*) You mean *you* are not in love with *me*. I know that. It doesn't matter so much, does it? There's always lust.

CLIVE: That's not a word Zane Grey uses.

ANN: I don't get everything out of books, Clive. I've got eyes —and a body under this puppy-fat.

CLIVE: You aren't fat, Ann. You're very pretty.

ANN: As pretty as the girls in Curzon Street?

CLIVE: I don't go to bed with the girls in Curzon Street.

ANN: Never?

CLIVE: I've done it. Two or three times, I suppose. When I've been fed up and alone.

ANN: You aren't alone now?

CLIVE: Yes. I'm very alone.

ANN: Well, then, why go to Curzon Street when there's me?

CLIVE: Lust isn't very strong, Ann, unless there's love, too. Curzon Street takes only half an hour. And there are twenty-four hours in a day.

ANN: We have things in common. Books.

CLIVE: *Riders of the Purple Sage* is a subject we might exhaust.

ANN: How cold and beastly you are.

CLIVE: Only sensible.

ANN: You'll be able to boast now, won't you, that you've had an immoral proposal from a girl of nineteen.

CLIVE: I'm not the boasting kind. I've been trained in a different school, Ann. You see, the first woman I loved was happily married.

ANN: Have you loved a lot of people?

CLIVE: Only four. It's not a high score at thirty-eight.

ANN: What happened to them, Clive?

CLIVE: In the end the husbands won.

ANN: Were they all married?

CLIVE: Yes.

ANN: Why do you choose married women?

CLIVE: I don't know. Perhaps I fall in love with experience.

ANN: One has to begin.

CLIVE: Perhaps I don't care for innocence. Perhaps I'm trying to repeat that first time. Perhaps it's envy of other men, and I want to prove myself better than they are. I don't know, Ann. But it's the school I've been brought up in. There are no girls of nineteen in my school. We don't throw the school cap over the windmill, and there are no lessons in "all for love and the world well lost."

ANN: You don't sound so happy in your school.

CLIVE: I hate the lessons, but I'm very good at them.

ANN: What lessons, Clive?

CLIVE: Oh, how to make a husband like you. How to stay in the same house as the two of them and not to mind that, when night comes, she'll pay you a short visit if the coast is clear and he'll sleep away the whole night beside her. Then, of course, there are all kinds of elementary lessons. On passports, hotel registers, and on times when it's necessary to take adjoining rooms. And how to postpone discovery in spite of those kind mutual friends whom you always meet at unlikely little hotels in the Midlands.

ANN: Does the husband always discover?

CLIVE: They always have. And then the worst lessons begin.

ANN: You mean—about divorce?

CLIVE: No. I've heard about divorce. I've never encountered it. In my case the husbands have always been complaisant. You see, they love their wives too much to leave them, so they say. I seem to have always had an eye for very lovable women.

ANN: I suppose I'm terribly young, Clive, but I don't understand.

CLIVE: And people would call me a cad for telling you.

ANN: I have to learn.

CLIVE: Don't marry an Englishman, Ann. Englishmen prefer their friends and their clubs to their wives, but they have great staying power and a great sense of duty. The lover relieves them of their duty. And then you see without that—trouble, a beautiful brother-and-sister relationship can develop. It's very touching. And so damned boring for the lover.

ANN: Are you in love now?

CLIVE: Yes.

ANN: And that's how it is?

CLIVE: I tell myself it can't happen that way again. I'll see that it won't happen that way.

ANN: You want to marry her?

CLIVE: Yes.

ANN: I wish you wouldn't tell her—whoever she is—about me.

CLIVE: I'll try not to. But, Ann, when you're in love, you don't have secrets.

ANN: I've proved that, haven't I? I'd better go and look at the tele after all. Are you coming, Clive?

CLIVE: No. His Master's Voice is bad enough. I can't bear His Master's Eye.

Mary enters.

MARY: You two still talking away?

ANN: About Zane Grey. You know it's my only subject, Mary. (*She leaves.*)

MARY: She's upset. Why did she stay behind, Clive?

CLIVE: Oh, you know what the young are like. A crisis.

MARY: Still worried about her puppy-fat?

CLIVE: Yes.

MARY: I wish I was her age.

CLIVE: I don't.

MARY: What do you think of Victor?

CLIVE: He's been very kind to me.

MARY: Why shouldn't he be? He has no suspicion.

CLIVE: Are you sure? I thought that cigar . . .

MARY: I know Victor.

CLIVE: Yes. Of course. I forgot that.

MARY: It was sweet of you to come.

CLIVE: I didn't want to.

MARY: It was necessary, Clive. If we are to see more of each other. Now he knows you, he won't worry.

CLIVE: That's kind of him.

MARY: He *is* kind, Clive. Why don't you like him?

CLIVE: Perhaps he'll grow on me in time. With his anecdotes. He has a great many.

MARY: They come his way.

CLIVE: He reminded me of my dentist. I'm sorry. Forgive me, Mary.

MARY: Why should I? He *is* a dentist.

CLIVE: Oh. You never told me that.

MARY: We haven't spoken of him much, have we? He's not been your favourite subject these few weeks. And it's not exactly a glamorous profession.

CLIVE: Who cares?

MARY: I didn't want you to laugh at him, that's all.

CLIVE: Are you so fond of him?

MARY: Yes. (*Pause.*)

CLIVE: When are we going to get some time together, Mary?

MARY: I only missed one day with you this week.

CLIVE: You know what I mean by time.

MARY: Dear, I promise. Sometime, somehow. But it's difficult. It wouldn't be safe in England.

CLIVE: I don't want to be safe.

MARY: But . . .

CLIVE: All right. We can go abroad.

MARY: I've spent my hundred pounds with the children.

CLIVE: So have I. But there are ways. I can fix it. Couldn't we . . . next week . . .

MARY: Sally comes back next week for half-term. I have to be here. Then there's a Dental Association dinner, and Victor would think it odd if I was away. I always go with him.

CLIVE: After that . . .

MARY: Robin's got to have three teeth out. Don't look angry. Even a dentist's child has tooth-trouble. And I have to take him.

CLIVE: Doesn't your husband pull them out?

MARY: Of course he doesn't.

CLIVE: Surely you could change that appointment?

MARY: You don't know how difficult appointments are. We'd have to wait a month for another.

CLIVE: And then, I suppose, it's almost time for Sally to come home again.

MARY: You shouldn't have chosen a woman with a family, Clive. My job is full time just as yours is. You can't pack up and go away whenever you like either.

CLIVE: All the same, I'd do it if you asked me to.

MARY (*sharply*): Perhaps children are more important than second-hand books. (*Pause.*) Clive, don't let's get angry with each other—not tonight. It's been so good seeing you here. In my home. It's as though our life together were really beginning.

CLIVE: Cosy evenings with the dentist!

MARY: Are you going to use that against me now? What's wrong with being a dentist? It's more useful than selling Zane Greys to teen-agers.

CLIVE: The teen-ager asked me to go away with her.

MARY: Ann!

CLIVE: Any time I liked. For as long as I liked.

MARY: What did you say?

CLIVE: Naturally I refused the invitation.

MARY: Poor Ann.

CLIVE: I also promised, if I could, to keep it secret. What liars and cheats love makes of us.

MARY: You should have said yes. There wouldn't be any complications with Ann. She wouldn't have to write postcards home and buy presents for the children. She wouldn't remember suddenly in the middle of dinner that she'd forgotten to buy a pair of football boots. She's free. Do you think I don't envy her? I even envy her virginity.

CLIVE: That's not important.

MARY: Oh yes, it is. Men are jealous of a past if there's nothing else to be jealous of. You need your bloody sign.

CLIVE: I need a few weeks' peace of mind. If you're with me, I can sleep because you are not with him.

MARY: I've told you over and over again—I've promised you—we haven't slept together for five years. But I have no sign to prove it.

CLIVE: After a dental dinner and a drink or two things happen . . .

MARY: When that dies out, Clive, it doesn't come back. And sooner or later it always dies. Even for us it would die in time. It dies quicker in a marriage, that's all. It's killed by the children, by the chars who give notice, by the price of meat.

CLIVE: If only you had separate rooms.

MARY: The space between the beds is just as wide as a passage.

CLIVE: When he wakes up you're the first thing he sees. I envy that.

MARY: I'm up first. Clive, I'd move into the spare room, but he'd notice it. Sometimes bed-time is the only chance we have to talk. Dentists are very busy men.

CLIVE: I need a chance, too.

MARY: What you and I talk about is so different. With Victor I talk about Sally's room which needs re-painting. Can we postpone it till the autumn? Her school report says she has a talent for music. Ought she to have extra lessons in the holidays? And then there's the dinner which went wrong. Too much garlic in the salad and the potatoes were undercooked. Clive, that's the sort of talk that kills desire. Only kindness grows in that soil.

CLIVE: A lot of kindness.

MARY: Yes. (*Robin's voice calling:* "Mother. Mother.") The show must be over.

CLIVE: So we can't be together because of the dental dinner? Is Victor speaking on the problems of tartar? Do you dance with the other dentists?

MARY: Clive, what makes you rough tonight?

CLIVE: Perhaps a trick cigar.

MARY: Or refusing an invitation to an adventure?

Robin's voice nearer: "Mother. Mother."

CLIVE: I want one week with you—I might be able to persuade you then.

MARY: Persuade me of what?

CLIVE: To marry me.

MARY: Yes. It's possible.

CLIVE: Or he might discover where we'd been.

MARY: Yes.

CLIVE: He'd divorce you, wouldn't he, if he knew?

MARY: How can I tell?

CLIVE: Or would you tell him how sorry you were and ask to be taken back to the twin bed?

MARY: I'd never say I was sorry. I love you, Clive.

Robin enters as they move towards each other.
Mary is quick to adapt her words, quicker than Clive could ever have been.

MARY: I really do love you for all the trouble you take to find Ann and me the cheapest books. We've ruined you between the two of us.

ROBIN: Mother, the tele's terrible tonight. Father says it's the x-ray next door.

MARY: That's your father's joke, dear. Mr. Saunders wouldn't have a patient at this hour.

ROBIN: He says Mr. Saunders works twenty-four hours a day because his patients are so rich. He won't take National Health.

MARY: Where are the others, Robin?

ROBIN: Oh, listening to something political.

MARY: Have you finished your homework, dear?

ROBIN: I can finish it in the morning.

MARY: Then be off to bed now. It's late.

ROBIN: You won't forget to say good night?

MARY: No.

ROBIN: Do you think . . . ?

MARY: It's too late to think. Off with you.

ROBIN: What does sesquioxide mean? It's in my French dictionary.

MARY: I don't know. What does the dictionary say it is in English?

ROBIN: It says in English it's sesquioxide.

Robin goes out again.

MARY: He and Victor have a lot in common. You see what I mean now, don't you? A moment ago I could have slept with you on the sofa. I don't mean sleep. I wanted to touch you. I wanted your mouth. Now . . . homework, Mr. Saunders's x-rays, tucking a child up in bed. Don't let's have a family, Clive, whatever happens.

CLIVE: I'd have liked your child.

MARY: That's what you think now. But love and marriage don't go together. Not our kind of love. Please, Clive, be patient. You don't believe how much I long to say, "All right, nothing else matters, we'll go away tomorrow, the first plane anywhere. I won't think about Robin or Victor or Sally's music lessons. I'll only think about me. Me."

23

CLIVE: Not me?

MARY: We'd be too close to know which was which.

CLIVE: Mary, come back to me tonight.

MARY: I can't. How can I?

CLIVE: Say you are taking the dog for a walk.

MARY: There is no dog. Only a cat. And cats take their own walks.

The door opens and Ann comes in. She realizes for the first time with whom Clive is in love.

ANN: I'm sorry. I didn't mean . . .

MARY: We were only talking about dogs and cats and who likes which.

ANN: The tele was in bad form tonight.

MARY: So Robin told us.

ANN (*with relief*): Oh, has he been here?

MARY: Yes. Surely he said good night to you?

Voices outside and the Howards and Victor enter.

VICTOR: One for the road. I insist. While I call a taxi.

MRS. HOWARD: We'll walk home. It's a fine night. Don't you agree, William?

HOWARD: Yes. Good for Ann's dieting, too.

VICTOR: All the more time for a Scotch.

MRS. HOWARD: Not for me.

MARY: Nor me.

Victor fetches the whisky from the sideboard on the dining side of the room. He can be seen pouring out and arranging the glasses on a tray. He shifts the position of one glass. There is something a little too studied about the arranging.

CLIVE (*to Ann*): I'll walk back with you if I may.

MARY (*quickly*): There's no need for you to go yet. It's only half-past ten.

CLIVE: I have to be up very early. I've got to finish cataloguing.

MARY: Surely you can choose your own time for that.

CLIVE: You wouldn't understand how important a bookseller's catalogue is.

ANN: It must be like writing a novel.

Victor returns with a tray of whisky.

CLIVE: Yes, I think it is. One has to know what to put in and what to leave out.

ANN: I'd love to see how you do it.

CLIVE (*his eye on Mary but his speech to Ann*): Come in to-morrow morning and I'll show you. You could help me a lot if it would amuse you.

ANN: I'd love to help you.

VICTOR: Take your glass, William.

Howard takes a quick look at the tray, takes two glasses, and hands one to Clive.

Victor's face shows dismay. He puts the tray down but doesn't take the third glass.

HOWARD: Here, Root.

CLIVE: Thanks.

HOWARD: Your health, Victor. An excellent whisky. Why aren't you drinking?

VICTOR (*picking up the third glass*): I'll join you in a moment. Got to say good night to Robin.

Victor starts, glass in hand, towards the sideboard, but Howard pursues him.

HOWARD: And health to our lovely hostess, Victor. You'll join us in that, surely.

VICTOR: I seem to have drowned this whisky. I'll get myself another.

HOWARD: I said a health to Mary, Victor. You can't refuse that. Drink up like a man.

Victor is cornered. He puts the glass to his mouth, but it is a trick dribbling glass and the whisky pours down his jacket.

HOWARD: Hoist with your own petard.

CLIVE: A dribbling glass now!

Everyone laughs except Mary and Clive, who watches her.

HOWARD: He meant that for you, Root. Have you ever thought of trying one of those glasses on a patient, Victor? It might make him laugh in the chair.

VICTOR: It's not my lucky evening. I think you and Mary conspired . . . (*He goes to the sideboard and pours himself another drink. Over his shoulder*:) The fact is I'm not appreciated, Root. Except by my son.

MARY: Won't the whisky stain?

VICTOR: There wasn't enough whisky in it, Mary. You know I wouldn't waste my good Black Label. Well, here's to the whole pack of you, laughing hyenas though you are. This one is an honest drink. I remember Lord Caton saying once, "I don't like that pink stuff you put in my glass. Why don't you give me a whisky? Alcohol kills germs." I said, "Lord Caton,

I've seen many people cock-eyed from whisky, but I've never known any cocci or streptococci, or even staphylococci killed by alcohol yet." Come along, one more for the road, both of you.

HOWARD: Not me. We've got to keep your hand steady for the sake of your patients. Come on, Margaret.

MRS. HOWARD: It's been a lovely evening. We were so glad, too, to have a chance of meeting Mr. Root. (*To Clive:*) Ann has talked about you so much.

CLIVE (*As Ann holds out her hand*): You forget. I'm coming with you.

ANN: Good night, Mrs. Rhodes. Thank you so much.

VICTOR: Coats this way. (*He leads the way out.*)

HOWARD: Victor's in good form. A cutlet with us next time, Mary.

CLIVE: Good night, Mrs. Rhodes, and thank you.

MARY: We'll see you again soon?

CLIVE: I may be going abroad for a while.

MARY: I'll drop in tomorrow morning

Only Ann is left in the doorway. She watches them.

CLIVE: Not in the morning. I'm cataloguing with Ann.

MARY: Oh yes. I forgot.

She watches him follow Ann out. She stands listening to the sound of good nights. A door closes. She goes to the window and, drawing the curtains apart, watches her guests depart— one of her guests at any rate. A key turns in the lock outside and then a bolt is thrust home. Victor is securing the house for the night. He comes in.

VICTOR: Windows locked?

MARY: Yes.

VICTOR: I think they enjoyed themselves.

MARY: Yes.

VICTOR: I liked your young friend, Root.

MARY: I'm glad.

VICTOR: So did Ann, I think. Ha, ha. (*He collects the glasses and carries them into the other half of the room.*) They'd make a good couple.

MARY: He's nearly twenty years older.

VICTOR: Well, I'm more than ten years older than you are. A difference like that gives a marriage stability. (*He goes to the window.*) This window's not locked. Are you sure yours are?

MARY: Yes.

He comes and tests them all the same.

VICTOR: Now did I, or did I not, lock the back door?

MARY: What are you afraid for, Victor? There's no old family silver.

VICTOR: Well, there's always a little cash lying around. And there's your fur coat.

MARY: The insurance is worth more than my old mink.

VICTOR: It's the idea of the thing, I suppose. (*He yawns and sits down on the sofa.*)

MARY: Tired?

VICTOR: A bit. (*Pause.*) You think I'm too careful about the house. But I'm not so careful as my father used to be. He always locked the inside doors too. Even the lavatory. He really believed it was all part of the Church of England because of that piece in the church service. You know—a strong man keeps his house.

MARY: There's something too about moths.

VICTOR: Oh, mothballs are your province. But I always believe that wearing clothes instead of storing them keeps the moths away.

MARY: I expect you're right.

VICTOR: The same applies to teeth.

MARY: How interesting.

VICTOR: Mary, is something wrong?

MARY: What could be? I clean my teeth twice a day.

VICTOR: I didn't mean your teeth.

MARY: I thought that was your chief interest.

VICTOR: Yes. After my family. Is that wrong? (*She doesn't reply.*) You weren't ashamed of marrying a dentist sixteen years ago.

MARY: I'm not ashamed, Victor. Not of you.

VICTOR: But people are. I don't know why. My patients don't ask us to dinner. Yet they ask their doctor. Though he deals in more ignoble parts of the body than I do.

MARY: I told you I'm not ashamed.

VICTOR: I wonder how many doctors could say they were as trained as I am. I have to know surgery, radiology, prosthesis . . .

MARY: What's prosthesis?

VICTOR: It's too late to tell you now.

MARY: It *is* late. Is your first appointment at nine?

VICTOR: Nine-thirty. There was a time, Mary, when you were interested in what I did.

MARY: Of course I'm interested.

VICTOR: Admit you aren't. There's nothing wrong in that. If those two young ones marry, you can be sure Ann won't be so interested in the bookshop after a few years. It's human nature, Mary. I used to enjoy shopping with you. I don't now. I get impatient when you can't decide about the new curtains. I feel out of place among the shop assistants—as you would feel in my surgery in town. We have different professions, Mary. For a year or two we want to share them, but we can't. I'm not a mother and you aren't a dentist. That's not a tragedy.

MARY: Who's talking about a tragedy?

VICTOR: It's not enough to break a marriage.

MARY: Of course not. Who said it was? What's the matter, Victor?

VICTOR: I've felt for the last month that you were unhappy. And now I've drunk enough to talk. We don't talk often.

MARY: I've been a little tired, that's all. The spring. It's always tiring.

VICTOR: You need a holiday without the children. While Sally's away.

MARY: It's difficult. There's half-term. And Robin's teeth.

VICTOR: We are both working too hard. We ought to go off somewhere—by ourselves. You and I haven't had a holiday together for a long time.

MARY (*flatly*): We haven't, have we?

VICTOR: The sooner the better for both of us. If only for a week. Suppose after Sally goes back—

MARY (*quickly*): There's the Dental Association dinner.

VICTOR: Oh yes. I'd forgotten. (*Doubtfully, asking her advice:*) I could miss it, couldn't I?

MARY: You never have.

VICTOR: I mustn't get too set in my ways.

MARY: It's the only time in the year you can meet Baxter and Saville.

VICTOR: A wife comes before old friends. You don't look well, Mary.

MARY: Suppose I went off for a few days on my own.

VICTOR (*with a cheerful laugh*): You'd be bored to death.

MARY: How do you know?

VICTOR: Well, I mean it's so unlike you.

MARY: I could go with someone.

VICTOR: Who?

MARY: Oh, somebody's sure to be free.

VICTOR: But you said just now how difficult it was to get away.

MARY: You don't need me at the dinner.

VICTOR: You always come.

MARY: I have old friends as well as you.

VICTOR: I offered not to go. Mary, it looks very much . . .

MARY: Yes?

VICTOR: As though you'd rather have a holiday without me.

MARY: That's stupid, Victor.

VICTOR: Then why shouldn't we both leave out the dinner?

MARY: You'd miss it, that's why. And when I'm tired like this I'm no companion, Victor.

VICTOR: Where did you think of going?

MARY: I don't know. Somewhere abroad—somewhere quiet. I could go with Jane. She never spends her allowance. We could manage on it for a week.

VICTOR: Have I ever met Jane?

MARY (*lying hard*): I think once.

VICTOR: I have an idea. (*He takes out his notebook to examine the dates.*) You could go away with what's-her-name—Jane—immediately after half-term, and then four days later I'd join you—after the dinner. Then I'd have both, the dinner and the holiday with you. Perhaps we could even get rid of Jane.

MARY (*desperately seeking a solution*): It doesn't seem fair to Jane. To come all that way—

VICTOR: What way?

MARY: From Northumberland.

VICTOR: Well then, why not take our holiday in Northumberland?

MARY: But I want sun, Victor, sun. We have enough rain here. And think how dreary it would be for Jane.

VICTOR: When did I meet Jane?

MARY: When we were married, I think. She never comes to London.

VICTOR: Just stays there in the rain? What's her other name?

MARY (*the first word that comes*): Crane.

VICTOR: Jane Crane stays in the rain. She sounds a bit lowering as a companion.

MARY: It wouldn't be much fun for you with her there.

VICTOR: Oh, I don't know. She'd be a companion for you while I was busy.

MARY: Busy at what?

VICTOR: That's another bright idea of mine. I've always wanted to see the Dutch dental hospitals. So you and Jane could go to Amsterdam.

MARY: It rains in Amsterdam.

VICTOR: Nonsense. It's called the Venice of the north.

MARY: I think that's Stockholm.

VICTOR: Well, let's go to Stockholm then. Swedish dentistry is just as interesting, and there's a special Scandinavian allowance for tourists.

MARY: I'd thought of some little place in the south. In the sun.

VICTOR: Oh, no, that wouldn't do at all. It would have to be a city because then I can get a business allowance. The three of us can't enjoy ourselves on Jane's hundred pounds.

MARY: I hadn't thought there would be three of us.

VICTOR: Be sensible, Mary. You'd be bored to death alone with Jane. You haven't seen her for years. So you say. You might not even like each other now. Early friends drop out like—like milk teeth.

MARY: Please, do you have to bring dentistry into everything?

VICTOR: You're behaving in a very odd way, Mary. Here I am proposing a holiday, trying to make the whole thing fun for you, and one would almost think I was forcing you to go away. Stockholm is one of the beauties of the north. There are lots of people who'd give their . . . (*He hesitates.*)

MARY: Eye teeth to see it.

VICTOR: The town hall is famous. And the glass.

MARY: The Royal Family is the most democratic in Europe. Please, Victor, if it has to be a city I'd rather go to Amsterdam.

VICTOR: Right. It was my first choice, too. Now let's look at dates. Sally goes back on the twelfth. There's no reason why you and Jane shouldn't leave on the thirteenth. My dinner's on the sixteenth. I could join you on the seventeenth.

MARY: Leave one day, Victor, for a hangover. You won't be in bed till two.

VICTOR: Right. Then I'll join you on the eighteenth. When does Robin have his teeth out?

MARY: Not till the twenty-fifth.

VICTOR: Splendid. We'll get a whole week together. And Jane may not want to stay as long as that.

MARY: I don't suppose she will. But there's Robin. We can't leave him all alone.

VICTOR: He can go to his aunt. Now don't think about it any more. My secretary can book the plane and the hotel rooms—the Amstel is the best. Is Jane a Miss or a Mrs.?

MARY (*hesitating*): Miss. Why?

VICTOR: The air company will want details of the names.

MARY (*seeing the complications ahead*): I'd rather go by boat. The sea air . . .

VICTOR: Two-berth cabin then?

MARY: Leave out the cabin. It's expensive.

VICTOR: Dear Mary, I hope I can still afford a cabin for my wife. Would you rather have two singles?

MARY: But, Victor, would you mind very much if I paid for myself—just this time?

VICTOR: But why?

MARY: I want it to be my present for Jane. She's not well off.

VICTOR: You know you'll be short before the end of the month.

MARY: If I am, then I'll come to you. (*The sound of Robin crying:* "Mother, Mother, Mother." *Wearily:*) I forgot to say good night.

VICTOR: Time for all of us to say good night.

MARY: You use the bathroom first. I want to write to Jane.

VICTOR: Why not wait till morning?

ROBIN'S VOICE: "Mother, Mother, Mother."

MARY (*shouts*): I'm coming, Robin. (*To Victor:*) I want to write while the idea's fresh. I won't be long.

Mary goes out. Victor looks around to see that everything is tidy. He straightens the cushions. As he does this to one of the chairs he remembers the musical box, and fetches it from where Mary had put it; he slips it again under the cushions. He sits down for a moment to try it out, a blissful look upon his face, and lets it play two bars. Then he gets up and puts out the light and goes into the other half of the room. There he locks the whisky in the sideboard cupboard. He turns out the lights there too and goes. Pause, and then Mary enters. She goes to a telephone and dials a number. After a while a voice answers.

MARY: Clive. Are you alone? . . . I'm coming away with you, Clive. . . . I only mean a holiday. Could you leave on the thirteenth? . . . No, we can't go there, it's too far for a short holiday, Clive. . . . But I can only manage four days. I'm sorry, but that's how things are. And, Clive, it's got to be Amsterdam. . . . I can't tell you why now. It just has to be, Clive. It's the Venice of the north. . . . All right. If you don't want four days alone with me in Amsterdam, just say so. We can call it off. . . . If it does rain, Clive, what does it matter? We'll just stay in bed, drinking Bols, whatever that is. . . . Oh, he's quite happy about it. He thinks I'm going with someone called Jane Crane. . . . No, she doesn't exist. . . . The name just came into my head. . . . What do you mean, "Jane, Jane, tall as a crane"? Why do you all have to make up verses about her? . . . I don't care if Edith Sitwell wrote them. I can't alter Jane's name now. . . . Clive, will you do the bookings? I'll pay you back, next month when my allowance comes in. Any hotel but the Amstel. . . . I know it's the best, but someone I know is arriving there on the eighteenth. I don't want them mixed up. . . . You are happy, darling? . . . Yes, I am. . . . No, we won't buy diamonds. . . . Did you say herrings? *Raw* herrings? . . . Oh, but I think raw herrings sound fascinating, and anything may happen, Clive, anything. Even in Amsterdam.

The curtain falls as she talks.

SCENE II

A hotel bedroom in Amsterdam. Two single beds have been pushed together to make a double. They are unmade. The room is that of a medium-priced hotel: a desk, one easy chair, a tall looking-glass in the wardrobe door, a door leading to the bathroom. The room is in the confusion of packing up. One man's incredibly shabby suitcase is already locked and ready by the door; two women's cases—very decorative—lie open in a froth of tissue paper beside the bed. The bathroom door is open and Mary speaks from inside to Clive, who is sitting glumly on the bed in his shirt-sleeves.

MARY'S VOICE: You haven't packed your face-cloth.

CLIVE: Never mind.

MARY'S VOICE: And there's a packet of razor blades here.

CLIVE: Let the valet have them.

MARY'S VOICE: Darling, do you always scatter your belongings over the globe like this?

CLIVE: How damnably cheerful you sound.

Mary comes to the door of the bathroom, her hands full of plastic pots and tubes. She is still in her dressing gown.

MARY: I've been happy, that's why. Haven't you?

CLIVE: Yes, in a way.

MARY: Is that all?

CLIVE: The first day I was happy. Even the second. Yesterday was not so good.

MARY: I loved yesterday.

CLIVE: The shadow of today was over it. But I didn't know then what a shadow. Mary, why didn't you tell me about Victor before we came away?

MARY: I was afraid you wouldn't come.

CLIVE: You could have told me yesterday.

MARY: And spoilt it all. All the lying late in bed, the wine we drank at lunch, even that silly film we saw . . .

CLIVE: Yes, you were happy, and all the time you were deceiving me.

MARY: I've been happy deceiving Victor, too, haven't I? You didn't mind me being happy doing that.

CLIVE: I understood our relationship was rather different.

MARY: Do you think I like packing up and going off to the Amstel to meet Victor?

CLIVE: He gets a whole week of you. I had three days.

MARY: It was the only way I could manage anything at all.

CLIVE: He fixed our holiday. Why didn't he fix our room at the Amstel too?

MARY: I told him Jane wanted somewhere small and quiet.

CLIVE: So he had our address all the time?

MARY: Something might have happened to the children. I had to be available.

CLIVE: Of course your room at the Amstel will be a much nicer one than this.

MARY: I've booked two single rooms, Clive.

CLIVE: And tonight I suppose you'll take him to that little restaurant by the canal . . . and that bar . . .

MARY: I won't take him anywhere we've been together.

CLIVE: There aren't so many good restaurants in Amsterdam, and Victor likes his food.

MARY: Darling, what's the great difference? If I weren't meeting him at the Amstel, I'd be meeting him at home tonight. I'm just meeting him, Clive, as one meets a kind relation and talks about the family.

CLIVE: This was our life here. We haven't had a very long one. Three days of birth, growing up, and I suppose this is age. Why had he got to butt into *our* life?

MARY: Some people might say you'd butted into his.

CLIVE: Oh, don't be so damnably fair-minded. Not today.

MARY (*on her knees by suitcase*): Clive, help me with this case.

CLIVE (*not looking at her*): What's wrong with the bloody case?

MARY: I can't make the key turn.

CLIVE: I suppose you've busted the lock.

MARY: Won't you help?

CLIVE: Why should I help you to go away from me? (*All the same he joins her.*) You shouldn't buy cases for looks. You ought to buy them for wear.

MARY: Yours hasn't worn so well.

CLIVE (*struggling with the key*): Anyway I don't go in for fancy monograms. M.R. for Mary Rhodes.

MARY: It could stand for Mary Root too. (*There is a ring at the door.*) Come in. Entrez. Whatever you call it.

39

The Hotel Valet enters.

VALET: Are your bags ready, Madam?

MARY: I won't be a minute.

CLIVE (*pointing to his case*): You can take that—the shabby one.

The Valet leaves with Clive's suitcase.

MARY: It's no use. The lock *is* broken.

CLIVE: I'll get you a strap.

MARY: Have you time before the plane?

CLIVE: I don't have to report for an hour. When do you have to report?

MARY: He's on the midday plane.

CLIVE: We may pass each other at the airport. Don't worry. I'll be ready to hide my face behind a newspaper.

MARY: You needn't. He wouldn't think there was anything wrong.

CLIVE: Is he as dumb as that?

MARY: It's not dumbness. When a man doesn't want a woman any more, he can't imagine anyone else desiring her—that's all.

Clive gets up.

CLIVE: I'll go and buy the strap. (*Mary remains squatting by the suitcase.*) Aren't you going to kiss me? For being obedient?

MARY: This isn't good-bye. Even at the air terminus it won't be good-bye. Clive, we're going to be together again. Over and over again. For years.

CLIVE: Are you sure?

MARY: Even if you told me you didn't want to go on, I wouldn't believe you. I have my proofs, Clive.

CLIVE: Where are they?

MARY: I can't show them to you now.

Pause.

CLIVE: I'll be back as quickly as I can.

When Clive has gone Mary busies herself packing again. Then she goes to the telephone.

MARY: Reception, please. (*There is a ring at the door.*) Entrez. Reception? This is room 121. Will you have my bill ready, please?

The door of the bedroom opens. Mary has her back to it as she telephones.
The Valet stands on one side to admit Victor, who is followed by a man in a Continental suit.

MARY: Yes. We're checking out in a few minutes. (*Over her shoulder to the Valet, her hand over the receiver.*) You can't take my bags yet. I'm waiting for a strap. (*To the Reception.*) Yes. We had breakfast this morning.

The Valet leaves.

VICTOR: Guess who's here!

MARY: Victor!

VICTOR: I thought you'd be surprised.

MARY: What are you doing here?

VICTOR: I was very careful at the dinner. I didn't have a hangover and I caught the night boat.

MARY: Why didn't you go to the Amstel?

VICTOR: I did, but you hadn't arrived. Anyway, it's such a huge place, Mary. I thought it'd be more fun being here. And Jane will be happier not moving.

MARY: Jane's gone home.

VICTOR: Oh, fine. Of course I'm sorry to have missed her.

MARY: You wouldn't be comfortable here, Victor. And I don't think they've got another room. Jane's was taken at once.

VICTOR: Oh, this is quite big enough for two. A fine big bed.

MARY: It's not really a double bed. I don't know why they arranged it this way. There's a nasty crack in the middle.

VICTOR: Oh well, we only need to pull the beds apart. Bathroom through there? (*He is already taking control of the room.*) Separate toilet—that's nice. What's the coffee like?

MARY (*weakly*): Good.

VICTOR: And the rolls?

MARY: They're good too.

VICTOR: Raw herrings. And cheese for breakfast. How it all comes back.

MARY: Comes back?

VICTOR: I used to know Amsterdam well when I was a student. I'll show you spots you won't have found with Jane. (*He sits on the bed and bumps up and down.*) Good mattress, too. This is much more sympathetic than the Amstel.

The Stranger coughs.

MARY (*helplessly*): Who's this man, Victor? Your bodyguard?

VICTOR: Oh, stupid of me. He was at the dinner. Dr. van Droog—my wife.

VAN DROOG (*bows, and says something rapidly in Dutch*): Buitengewoon aangenaam met Uw charmante echtgenote te ontmoeten.

MARY: Dinner?

VICTOR: The dental dinner. We travelled across together. Dr. van Droog is one of the biggest manufacturers of dental instruments in Holland. The trouble is he doesn't speak any English.

MARY: You must have had a very gay dinner. But why bring him here?

VICTOR: He's staying here.

MARY: You don't mean with us?

VICTOR: No, no. He always stays here on his way to The Hague.

VAN DROOG: Het was my zeer aangenaam Uw echtgenoot te ontmoeten, en in elk gewal wat hartelijkheid te kunnen uitwisselen, daar wij bij gebrek aan een gemeenschappelijke taal helaas niet van gedachten kunnen wisselen.

MARY: What's he saying?

VICTOR: I don't fully understand.

VAN DROOG: Het was mij een eer de gast te zijn van de Dental Association of Great Britain.

VICTOR: It may be important. Ring for the valet.

MARY: The valet? (*She rings obediently.*)

VICTOR: To translate, of course.

VAN DROOG: Neemt U my niet kwalyk dat ik geen Engels ken.

A ring at the door.

VICTOR: Entrez.

The Valet enters and goes for the bags.

VICTOR (*now in charge of the situation*): No. Not the bags. I want you to translate what this gentleman has to say.

VALET (*in Dutch*): Hy wil dat ik het vertaal, Mijnheer.

VAN DROOG (*rapidly*): Zeg aan Mijnheer, dat het mij zeer aangenaam is, met zijn vrouw kennis te maken.

43

VALET: He says it is a great pleasure, sir, to him to have met your wife. (*To Dr. van Droog:*) Waar ontmoette U de vrouw van deze heer?

VICTOR: What are you saying?

VALET: I am asking him, sir, where he had the pleasure of meeting your wife.

VICTOR: Here, of course. Where do you think? This is my wife.

VALET (*looking at Mary reproachfully*): I see. I did not understand. I am sorry.

VAN DROOG: Wilt U aan Mevrouw zeggen dat ofschoon, ik geen Engles spreek, ik er veel van kan verstaan, als men langzaam sprekt.

VALET: He wants me to tell your wife that though he cannot speak English he can understand a lot if you speak very slowly.

MARY: That's certainly going to be fun. Victor, would you mind going away for a few minutes—to the bar, anywhere, with Dr. van Droog. I have to get dressed and go and find a strap for my bag.

VICTOR: There's no hurry for that now. We're staying here.

VAN DROOG: Het zou mij een groot genoegen doen, als Mijnheer en Mevrouw Rhodes mijn gasten willen zijn in mijn fabriek in den Haag. Het is een zeer moderne fabriek, en ik heb een nieuw ontwerp voor een dril, die beter is dan de Duitse.

VALET: The gentleman says he would be delighted if the two of you would be his guests at his factory at The Hague. He says it is very up to date and he has a new—(*the Valet hesitates, not knowing the word in English*)—a new, better than the German, a new . . .

VICTOR: New what?

The Valet puts his finger in his mouth and imitates the sound of a drill.

MARY: Vivid. Only you left out the spasm of pain. Victor, please go. Just for a few minutes while I get dressed. (*She is watching the door anxiously.*)

VICTOR: A moment, and I'll get rid of him for you. Must be polite. (*To the Valet:*) Will you explain to Dr. van Droog that we shall be delighted to visit his factory. I am looking particularly for some new instruments for gingivectomy.

VALET: For what, sir?

VICTOR: For gingivectomy.

MARY: I'm not going to stand here in my dressing-gown, half naked, while you discuss ginger-something with Dr.— Dr.—

VALET: I do not know the word in Dutch, sir.

MARY: Take him away, Victor, or I'll push him out.

Mary makes a gesture with her hand, but Dr. van Droog seizes it and holds her firmly while he makes her a speech in Dutch.

VAN DROOG: Ik ben zo verheugd dat U myn uitnodiging aange-nomen heeft. Myn collega's en ik zien Uw bezoek met ongeduld tegemoet.

In the middle of the speech the door opens and Clive enters. Mary has her back turned while she listens to Dr. van Droog. Victor sits on the bed facing the door. He smiles brightly at Clive.

VICTOR: How are you, Root? Nice to see you.

Mary turns quickly, but even more disconcerned than Mary is the Valet.

CLIVE (*awkwardly*): I didn't know you were here.

VICTOR: Just moved in.

CLIVE: I thought you were going to the Amstel.

VICTOR: It's better here. There's a sort of holiday feeling about this place. What are you doing in Amsterdam?

CLIVE: I was getting a strap. For this suitcase.

MARY (*coming to the rescue*): Clive's been buying books. It was such a surprise when Jane and I ran into him. He's been very kind to Jane.

VICTOR: This is Dr. van Droog, a neighbour of ours at home, Mr. Clive Root. (*To the Valet:*) Go on. Translate.

VALET (*translating unwillingly*): Dit is onze buurman in Engeland.

Dr. van Droog bows and replies in Dutch.

VAN DROOG: Zeer aangenaam, U te ontmoeten. Ik hoop dat U de professor en zyn echtgenote wilt vergezellen naar den Haag om myn fabriek van tandeheelkundige instrumenten te bezichtigen.

VALET (*wearily*): Dr. van Droog welcomes you to the city of Amsterdam and hopes you will accompany the Professor and his wife to The Hague to see over his manufactury of dental appliances.

VICTOR: Good idea, Root. Come along with us.

CLIVE: I'm leaving today.

VICTOR: The books can wait. Stay and keep my wife company while I'm doing the clinics. Know Amsterdam well?

CLIVE: My first visit.

VICTOR: I'll show you around then. There's a little restaurant—by the canal—if it's still there . . .

CLIVE (*watching Mary*): It's still there. I know the one you mean.

VICTOR: They used to do wonderful chickens on a spit.

CLIVE: The spit still turns.

VICTOR: Talking of spit . . . (*To the Valet:*) Ask Dr. van Droog what one has to pay here for absorbent wools. By the gross, of course.

VALET: Please, I do not know the Dutch . . . please . . .

CLIVE (*to Mary*): I hope this strap will do. (*He drops it on the suitcase and prepares to go.*)

MARY: Where are you going?

CLIVE: Home.

MARY: You don't have to be at the airport yet. There were those books we had to talk about.

VICTOR: Oh, if you're going to talk about books I'm off. With Dr. van Droog.

Victor takes Dr. van Droog's arm, but Dr. van Droog begins to talk rapidly again in Dutch.

VAN DROOG: Bent U ooit in India geweest?

VALET (*patiently*): Dr. van Droog wants to know whether you have ever visited India.

CLIVE: No. I haven't. Why?

VALET (*to Dr. van Droog*): Neen.

VAN DROOG (*to Valet*): Zeg aan Mynheer dat zyn voornaam my interesseert. Is hy misschien een afstammeling van de beroemde Robert Clive?

VALET (*to Clive*): Dr. van Droog is interested in your pre-name. He thinks you are perhaps an ancestor of the great Robert Clive.

VICTOR: Descendant.

CLIVE: No.

VALET (*to Dr. van Droog*): Neen.

MARY: Victor. Please, Victor.

Victor at last succeeds in getting Dr. van Droog through the door.

VICTOR: We'll be waiting in the bar. Don't be long.

He goes. The Valet follows and closes the door.

CLIVE: Who in God's name is that man?

MARY: Why *are* you called Clive?

CLIVE: My father was a great admirer of his. To the point of imitation.

MARY: Imitation?

CLIVE: He shot himself. Like Clive. From a sense of failure. It's not a bad reason. So now the family is reunited—here. Has Victor decided on which side of the bed he is going to sleep?

MARY: I've got to dress. (*She breaks away and goes to the bathroom.*)

CLIVE: He likes to give the final turn of the screw, doesn't he? He's not satisfied with moving into our room and our bed. He has to make it a cheap farce with his Dutch manufacturer of dental instruments. We aren't allowed a tragedy nowadays without a banana skin to slip on and make it funny. But it hurts just the same.

MARY (*coming to the door without her dressing-gown*): What? What were you saying about banana skin?

CLIVE: Nothing that mattered. It can hurt just as much as the great Clive's bullet, that's all.

MARY: What's banana skin got to do with it?

CLIVE: Oh, forget the banana skin. It's Victor. Victor coming here. Where we made love.

MARY: That's not Victor's fault. He doesn't know.

CLIVE: Doesn't he? I *happen* to be in Amsterdam—I *happen* to walk into your bedroom before you are dressed. But oh, no, Victor's a damned wise monkey. He sees no evil, thinks no evil.

MARY: That's not a bad quality.

CLIVE: You always leap to his defence, don't you? If you love him so much, why did you come away with me?

MARY: There are different kinds of love.

CLIVE: Oh, yes, the higher and the lower. And I'm the lower.

MARY: I didn't say so. Clive, how many times do I have to swear to you that Victor and I aren't lovers? We aren't man and wife in that way. Why won't you believe me?

CLIVE: Go and look in the glass before you put your frock on. Then you'll know why. I'll never believe you, Mary, until you sleep beside me every night.

MARY: You haven't children.

CLIVE: A loveless marriage isn't good for children, so the *Sunday Mirror* says.

MARY: But you see, Clive, this isn't a loveless marriage.

CLIVE: Yes, I do see.

Mary goes back into the bathroom to put on her frock. Clive takes a small package out of his pocket and puts it on the dressing table. He is moving to the door when Mary calls to him.

MARY'S VOICE: What are you doing, Clive?

CLIVE: Catching my plane.

Mary comes back with her frock on.

MARY: Why don't you stay, as Victor asked?

CLIVE: Good God, do you really expect me to take the next-door room . . . ?

MARY: Victor's going to be busy all day.

CLIVE: Mary, you're either the most immoral woman I've ever known—or the most innocent.

Mary takes up the package.

MARY: What's this, Clive?

CLIVE: A present I meant to give you when we got past the Customs.

MARY (*excited and beginning to unwrap it*): Clive!

CLIVE: You'll have to take it through yourself now—or get Victor to hide it among the absorbent wool rolls.

MARY (*opening a box*): Ear-rings. But they're diamonds, Clive.

CLIVE: This is the city for diamonds.

MARY: You can't possibly afford—

CLIVE: They're the profit on one fine copy of Redouté's *Lilies*.

MARY: But the currency . . . This couldn't have come out of your hundred pounds.

50

CLIVE: There are always ways. I went to a little man in Knightsbridge. There are quacks nowadays for every known disease—even for a collapsed currency. The currency quacks are especially smart. They have deep carpets and the receptionists are sexy and frankly impertinent because they think you may be a film magnate.

MARY: Why a film magnate?

CLIVE: All film magnates suffer from collapsed currencies. It's rather like visiting a fashionable abortionist.

MARY: You could go to prison for this.

CLIVE: So could he. Everything is on trust between two crooks. No letters. No cheques. Just cash and guarded telephone calls naming no names. Of course this was a very small transaction. He wouldn't have bothered with it if I hadn't had a good introduction.

MARY: Who from?

CLIVE: A film magnate who happens to read books. Erotica, of course.

MARY: Clive, they're lovely. But I don't need presents from you.

CLIVE: I would rather have given you a plain gold ring.

MARY: You know I want the plain gold ring.

CLIVE: I wish you would show it in the usual simple way.

MARY: What's that?

CLIVE: Leave your husband and marry your lover.

MARY: Do you call that simple?

CLIVE: Hundreds of people do it every year.

MARY: Perhaps they're tougher than I am, then. I've known you for less than two months, and I've known Victor for sixteen years. He's never been unkind even when I've run up bills. He's a good father. The children love him. Particularly Robin. It wasn't his fault we stopped—sleeping together. I warned you before, Clive—marriage kills that.

CLIVE: It can't go on like this, Mary. Odd days arranged by Victor. You have to choose.

MARY: And if I won't choose?

CLIVE: I'll leave you.

MARY: Do you mean that?

CLIVE: Yes.

MARY: And go off with that little bitch from the bank?

CLIVE: Perhaps. I hadn't thought of it.

MARY: You're so free, aren't you? You don't have to choose. You don't have to go to someone you love and say, "I'm leaving you. After sixteen years I'm leaving you for a man I've slept with for a month. You'll have to see to things for yourself—the dentist for Robin and writing to Matron about Sally, booking rooms for the seaside in August and getting all those damned little objects for the stockings in time for Christmas." I'm married, Clive. You aren't. You are a foreigner. Even when I sleep with you you are a foreigner.

CLIVE: If we were married—

MARY: You don't want that sort of marriage and I don't. You only marry that way once, and you've never tried.

CLIVE: Oh, yes, I've tried.

MARY: You want to be a lover with a licence, that's all. All right. You win. I'll leave Victor, but not just yet, Clive. Not

52

before Christmas. Please not before Christmas. Be patient until January, Clive.

CLIVE: I'd wait for longer than that if you'd promise—

MARY: Couldn't we wait till he finds out? He's sure to find out sooner or later.

CLIVE: He has a wonderful capacity for not noticing.

MARY: If he found out he wouldn't want me to stay, would he? There wouldn't be a struggle, or a choice. He'd throw me out. Say you'll wait till then, Clive.

CLIVE: Just now you only asked me to wait till January.

MARY: Perhaps he'll find out long before then.

CLIVE (*an idea has been born*): It's possible.

MARY: Just give me time. You gave me the ear-rings. Give me time too. Till he finds out.

CLIVE: Till he finds out.

MARY: I must go down, Clive. It's all right, isn't it, now?

CLIVE: Yes, it's all right.

MARY: And we'll see each other next week?

CLIVE: Of course. Won't you put on your ear-rings?

MARY: I'd better not. Not just yet. He might notice.

CLIVE: I see. Good-bye, Mary.

MARY: Until next week?

CLIVE: Until next week.

MARY: Aren't you coming down?

CLIVE: I'd rather not see Victor for a while if you don't mind.

MARY: He'll think it odd your staying up here.

CLIVE: Tell him I asked if I could use your desk to write a letter. I shan't be here long.

MARY: Au revoir, darling.

She touches the bed with her hand as she leaves.
Clive waits a moment and then goes to the desk and takes out notepaper and envelope. He unscrews his pen and on the point of writing stops and rings the bell.
After a pause the Valet enters.

VALET: Yes, sir? Can I take the bags now?

CLIVE: No. The lady is staying here. Do you want to earn fifty guilder?

VALET: Well, sir, naturally, but—

CLIVE: You have only to write a letter for me. I'll dictate it.

VALET: What kind of letter, sir?

CLIVE: Shall we say a hundred guilder and no questions?

VALET: As you please, sir.

CLIVE: Then sit down. (*The Valet sits.*) Here is a pen. Begin "Dear Mr. Rhodes"—no, make it Dear Sir. "I am the valet who looked after you in room 121." Got that?

VALET: Yes, sir.

CLIVE: "I am sorry to see a gentleman like you so sadly deceived."

VALET: How do you spell "deceived," sir?

CLIVE: Spell it any way you like. It will look more convincing.

VALET (*spelling out*): D-e-s-s-e-v-e-d.

CLIVE: Good enough. "A beautiful woman your wife—"

54

The door opens and Victor enters. The Valet looks nervously up, and stands. He is completely confused.

VICTOR: Mary here?

CLIVE: She went down to find you. I asked if I could use your desk—and your valet.

VICTOR: Why the valet?

CLIVE: I have to write a bread-and-butter letter in Dutch.

VICTOR: Well, make yourself at home, old chap. Make yourself at home.

CLIVE: Thank you.

VICTOR: Carry on. Don't mind me. Just going to wash.

Victor goes to the bathroom and begins running water. It has a proprietary sound which infuriates Clive.

CLIVE (*to Valet*): Sit down. (*The poor man is hopelessly confused but he obeys.*) "I have so much enjoyed my stay with you." (*Valet hesitates.*) Go on. "The windmills were just as I'd always imagined them."

The Valet writes. Victor emerges, drying his hands.

VICTOR: Just going to take my wife shopping. I've managed to lose Dr. van Droog. See you in London.

CLIVE: Give Mary my love.

VICTOR: Right you are. (*He pauses at the bed and picks up the bed-clothes.*) Can't say I like sleeping under these. I like good English blankets. Good-bye, Root.

CLIVE: Good-bye. (*Victor leaves. Clive turns to the Valet.*) Go on now with the letter. "I am sorry to see—" No, we've done that. "I feel that it is my duty to tell you . . . that before your arrival . . . your wife was sharing Room 121 . . . for four days . . . with the gentleman who went out to buy a strap. They had behaved very intimately together . . . and I am quite ready to be a witness in any proceedings . . ." (*The Valet looks up.*) Spell it how you like . . . "that you may wish to take. Your humble servant . . ." Now sign it, and post it a week today.

VALET: Shall I read it to you, sir?

CLIVE: No. I don't want any more to do with the beastly thing. Address the envelope to Victor Rhodes, Esq., 18 South Heath Lane, London, N.W., England.

Dr. van Droog puts his head inside the door and speaks in Dutch.

VAN DROOG: Het spyt my ik ben Mr. en Mrs. Rhodes kwytgeraakt?

VALET (*getting to his feet*) : He wishes to know where is Mr. and Mrs. Rhodes. I do not know who he is. I do not know who you are. I do not understand this (*indicating the letter*). I do not understand one damned thing.

Act

Two

The same scene as Act I, Scene I, about five-thirty of a warm sunny evening.

The sitting room is empty, but glasses for cocktails have been laid out on the dining-room table.

Robin's voice calling: "Mother, Mother."

Mary enters the dining room carrying bottles. She is wearing the new ear-rings. The voice goes on calling, "Mother," but she pays no attention, counting and marshalling the glasses: it is the eternal background noise of her life at home.

Robin enters the drawing room through the garden window, then shouts again.

ROBIN: Mother.

MARY: If you want to speak to me come where you don't have to shout.

ROBIN (*between the rooms*): What's the capital of Madagascar?

MARY: Antananarivo.

ROBIN: Thanks. What's a prime number?

MARY: A number that you can't divide into equal parts.

ROBIN: Thanks. What's Tio Pepe?

MARY (*looking at the bottle in her hand*): Sherry.

ROBIN: Tio means ten in Swedish.

MARY: Thanks.

57

ROBIN: There's a stamp I haven't got on one of Father's letters.

MARY: What kind?

ROBIN: Dutch. A new issue.

MARY: I suppose that will be from Dr. van Droog. I wonder who we can get to translate it.

ROBIN: Can I peel the stamp off? It's on the hall table.

MARY: Not until your father's opened the letter.

ROBIN: Who's coming to the party?

MARY: Mr. Root and the Howards—the Morgans, the Forsters, I think. I can't remember.

ROBIN: Is Ann coming?

MARY: I suppose so.

ROBIN: Do you think she'd like an electronic eye? I made one yesterday.

MARY: It would be an improvement on a stuffed mouse. Help me carry in some of these glasses, and I want to shift some tables into the garden. We've got to spread the party. Don't take too many at a time.

Robin follows her into the sitting-room, carrying glasses. During the ensuing dialogue they also carry one or two small tables through the garden windows.

ROBIN: Is Jane Crane coming?

MARY: No. Why?

ROBIN: It'd be just interesting to see her. None of us have.

MARY: She went straight home by train.

ROBIN: Jane Crane went home by train. She'll never be seen here ever again.

MARY: Why does everybody have to make up rhymes about her? It's quite an ordinary name, isn't it?

ROBIN: Not a *very* ordinary name. Did she like Amsterdam?

MARY: Of course. Why?

ROBIN: What did you do all day?

MARY: Why we—we looked at museums and things.

ROBIN: That sounds pretty dreary. You must have been glad when Father came.

MARY: Of course.

ROBIN: Did Father like Jane Crane?

MARY: They never met.

ROBIN: She *is* a mystery woman, isn't she? Nobody's met her except you.

MARY: And Mr. Root.

ROBIN: Oh, was he in Amsterdam too?

MARY: Yes.

ROBIN: Ann's got a crush on him.

MARY: How do you know?

ROBIN: I saw them on the heath while you were away. They looked as if they were in an about-to-take-hands condition. It would be terrible, wouldn't it, if they married.

MARY: For goodness' sake stop talking about things you don't understand.

Victor enters. He carries the afternoon post in his hand.

VICTOR: Sorry I'm too late to help. Who's coming?

MARY: The usual people. Had a bad afternoon?

59

VICTOR: Four fillings, three scalings, and one extraction.

ROBIN: Did you use gas?

VICTOR: Pentothal. (*He sits heavily down on the sofa.*) The new girl makes everything twice as long. She has no sense of order.

ROBIN: What kind of fillings were they, Father?

MARY: Don't worry your father. He's tired. Have you done your homework?

VICTOR: One porcelain and three amalgams.

ROBIN: Don't you ever use gold now?

VICTOR: Thank God, gold foil is out of fashion. It took five times as long.

ROBIN: Why?

MARY: Robin, I said homework.

ROBIN (*disgruntled*): Oh, all right. (*He goes.*)

MARY: He's at a tiresome age.

VICTOR: Oh, I think he was really interested. It would be amusing, wouldn't it, to have a dentist son?

MARY: Would it?

VICTOR: I could take him into partnership before I retired.

MARY: And you could consult each other at meals.

VICTOR: Yes. (*He notices the irony too late.*) What's wrong, Mary?

MARY: Nothing. Read your mail.

During the ensuing dialogue Mary moves with glasses and bottles between the two sections of the room and the garden.

VICTOR: There's nothing interesting. Two bills. Three catalogues and a letter from Dr. van Droog.

MARY: It is from Dr. van Droog?

VICTOR: It must be. He's the only man I know in Holland.

MARY: Robin wants the stamp.

VICTOR: He could have taken it.

MARY: I told him not to, until you'd read the letter.

VICTOR: Not much good reading it. It'd be double-Dutch to
me. (*He opens one of the catalogues.*)

MARY: That was a terrible day at The Hague. Except for the
Bols. I drank four glasses. I simply had to.

VICTOR: I don't know. It wasn't so bad, was it? The supersonic
drill was interesting. True, I didn't take to it much. That jet
of water playing on the patient's tooth to keep it cool—I'd be
afraid of not seeing the way and cutting the nerve.

MARY: Victor, can't you leave dentistry behind in the surgery
just for a little?

VICTOR: I'm sorry, Mary. You see, it's my life. (*He opens another catalogue.*) Even my letters are dental. What does a
dentist do when he retires? He can hardly write his memoirs.
The patients wouldn't like it.

MARY: He has to fall back on a hobby like other people.

VICTOR: You don't much care for my hobby, do you? You
know that shop in Oxford Street. I saw a wonderful rat there
the other day. Beautifully made, real craftsmanship. You make
it lurk in the shadows of the room. (*He throws down the
catalogue.*) Oh God, I'm feeling tired today. Well, here's for
Dr. van Droog. Why are there so many g's in the Dutch language?

Victor opens the letter with the Dutch stamp.
Mary goes into the dining room and begins to decant some
whisky.
Victor puts the letter on his knee, then picks it up and reads it
again.

MARY (*from the other room*): Why don't you go to bed? I'll
tell them the truth and say you're tired. When they've gone I'll
bring you up a tray. It's a cold meal anyway. (*Victor, with sud-*
den decision, tears the letter in two and drops it on the sofa.)
What about it, dear?

VICTOR: No. I'll stay.

Pause.

MARY (*from the other room*): Did you remember to write to
Sally for her birthday?

VICTOR: Yes.

MARY (*from the other room*): We've only got one bottle of
sherry, but the men will take whisky, won't they, or martinis?
Let me make the martinis if you're tired. (*She comes into the*
living room with a cocktail shaker.) Poor dear. You do look
all in.

VICTOR: Is Root coming?

MARY: Yes, I think so. Why? He was so kind, you know, to
Jane. Took her round to museums and art galleries—all the
places that bore me. We need more ash-trays. (*She is quite*
unconscious of the situation and the effect of her words on
Victor.) Did I tell you I got a letter from Jane this morning?
She's so sorry that she missed you in Amsterdam. Now there she
is, back in the frozen north. She's quite a hermit, but perhaps
she'll come to London after Christmas and then you'll meet her.

VICTOR (*who can bear no more*): It seems unlikely.

MARY: Unlikely?

VICTOR: Mary, was Root sleeping with you in Amsterdam?

A long pause.

MARY: Yes.

VICTOR: It was stupid of me not to guess. You married a stupid man.

MARY: You aren't stupid, Victor. I was beastly and clever with my lies. I hated them.

VICTOR: I suppose I ought to be glad the lies are over, but I'm not. I just don't know how to take the truth.

MARY: How did you find out?

VICTOR: This letter. From the valet in the hotel.

MARY: The valet!

VICTOR: A bit sordid, isn't it?

MARY: You tore it up.

VICTOR: I thought for a moment I could pretend it hadn't come. But I'm not strong enough. And what's the use of my lying, too?

MARY: Let me see it.

VICTOR: I'll read it to you if you like. It's in English. (*He puts the two pieces of the letter together.*) "Dear sir, I am the valet who looked after you in room 121." You remember the man. He translated for Dr. van Droog. "I am sorry to see a gentleman like you so sadly deceived." His spelling is not very good. "A beautiful woman your wife . . ."

MARY: What a foul letter.

VICTOR: It gets a bit confused here. I don't know what he means. He writes, "I have so much enjoyed my stay with you. The windmills were just as I always imagined them."

MARY: He must be mad.

VICTOR: What difference does it make? You said you slept with Root. He goes on, "I feel it is my duty to tell you that before your arrival your wife was sharing room 121." I don't have to read any more, do I?

MARY: No.

VICTOR: Are those his ear-rings you are wearing?

MARY: Yes.

VICTOR: An expensive present. I couldn't buy you much on my ten-pounds-a-day allowance. He seems to know the ropes better than I do.

MARY: He went to a black marketeer in Knightsbridge. A currency specialist.

VICTOR: It's the only romantic thing a man can do in these days, risk prison for a woman. I can't even do that. I'm a father. I can only give you a scarf with a map of Amsterdam on it. They look as though they're good diamonds.

MARY: You talk as though he bought me.

VICTOR: He did buy you. He bought you with novelty, anecdotes you hadn't heard before, books instead of teeth. I know what you think of my job. You didn't feel that way when we started. You used to talk quite poetically about dentistry. Only you called it "curing pain."

MARY: You are causing it now.

VICTOR: Me causing it? I remember a poem by Swinburne about a woman who loved a leper and washed his sores with her hair. Is it so much more difficult to love a dentist?

MARY: There never was such a woman. Or if there was it didn't happen that way. The sores would have got on her nerves very soon.

VICTOR: Like my dentist's chair?

MARY: Like your rat and your burning cigar and your dribbling glass. Victor, I'm sorry. I don't want to be angry. I don't know why I am. It's you who ought to be angry.

VICTOR: I was angry just now, but I couldn't keep it up. What are you going to do?

MARY: I wasn't planning to do anything until you found out.

VICTOR (*getting up from the sofa*): I wish I hadn't. Oh, how I wish I hadn't. If that damned valet hadn't written . . . Does Root want to marry you?

MARY: Yes.

VICTOR: Do you want to marry him?

MARY: I want to be with him, when I can, as much as I can.

VICTOR: That wasn't what I asked.

MARY: I never thought about marriage until he talked about it.

VICTOR: Don't think about it now. Mary, marriage isn't the answer. First editions can be just as boring in time as dentist's drills. He'll have his hobbies, too, and you won't care for them in a year or two. The trouble about marriage is, it's a damned boring condition even with a lover.

MARY: I didn't know you'd been bored too.

VICTOR: I can put up with any amount of boredom because I love you. It's the way of life that's boring, not you. Do you

65

think I'm never bored with people's teeth? One has to put up with it. Boredom is not a good reason for changing a profession or a marriage.

MARY: We haven't been married properly for years.

VICTOR: Oh, yes, we have. Marriage is living in the same house with someone you love. I never stopped loving you—I only stopped giving you pleasure. And when that happened I didn't want you any more. I wasn't going to use you like a pick-up in the park.

MARY: How did you know that?

VICTOR: You were always very quiet when we made love, but you had one habit you didn't know yourself. In the old days just before going to sleep, if you had been satisfied, you would touch my face and say, "Thank you." And then a time came when I realized that for months you had said nothing. You had only touched my face. (*In sudden pain:*) Do you say thank you to Root?

MARY: I don't know. Perhaps.

VICTOR: You are always so damnably honest—that's the awful thing about you.

MARY: What do you want me to say, Victor?

VICTOR: I want you to make absurd promises, to say you'll give him up, I want you to lie to me, but it never even occurs to you to pretend. You never pretended even in bed. It was thank you or nothing.

MARY: I never knew you noticed so much.

VICTOR: I'm not more stupid than other men.

MARY: You are talking to me as though I was a woman, and not just your wife. Do I have to sleep with another man before you do that?

66

Robin's Voice with its maddening wail: "Mother, Mother."

VICTOR: You'd better go to him.

MARY: I promised nothing.

VICTOR: I meant Robin.

MARY: He can wait. He only wants help with his homework.

VICTOR: We are all of us asking you for help, aren't we? Poor Mary. (*Robin's Voice:* "Mother. Mother.") How I wish all those people weren't coming.

MARY: It's too late to stop them now. It's a wonder the Howards aren't here already. They're always so punctual.

VICTOR: Mary, what do I say to Root? How do I behave in front of them? They don't know, but he does. How does a cuckold meet a lover the first time? It's funny how even now I depend on your advice.

MARY: I can't advise you.

VICTOR: You chose the furniture, you chose my shirts and my ties. I bring you patterns of my suits. You've always chosen for me. I'm lost when I'm not in my surgery. Mary, I can't live in a surgery.

ROBIN'S VOICE: Mother. Mother.

MARY: I'll have to go. He won't stop until I do.

VICTOR: Mary, please stay with me.

MARY: Don't make me choose. I can't choose. (*Robin's Voice:* "Mother.") I'll have to go.

As Mary passes him Victor clutches her arm.

VICTOR: Have I got to meet him?

MARY: I can't put him off now.

VICTOR: I'm just not accustomed . . . I need you, Mary.

67

MARY: So does he.

VICTOR: He hasn't sixteen years of habit behind him.

Mary goes. Victor stands for a moment; then without thinking what he is doing he collapses on to the musical chair and puts his face in his hands.
The chair starts playing "Auld Lang Syne," but Victor doesn't hear. He is crying behind his hands.
As the music grinds to a close Mary returns.

MARY: What on earth . . . ? (*The music stops. She goes to him and tries to pull his hands away, but he is ashamed of his tears.*) Victor, please, Victor. Be angry. I'm an unfaithful wife. Victor. (*She kneels beside him.*) You have to divorce me. Please do something, Victor. I can't.

VICTOR (*taking his hands from his face*): I'm sorry. The new girl, she's so careless. No oil of cloves. No guttapercha. It's been a bad day at the surgery. Just give me time to think.

The front door bell rings and Mary rises to her feet to go and greet her guests. The first to enter is Clive. Victor rises reluctantly. Both are at a loss.

CLIVE: Good evening.

VICTOR: Good evening.

CLIVE: I hope you had a good time in Amsterdam.

A pause.

VICTOR (*pulling himself together*): Oh, for me, you know, it wasn't altogether a holiday. Work. There's always work. Sit down. Would you like a whisky or shall I mix you a dry martini? I make good dry martinis.

The bell is ringing again as the curtain falls.

The same scene about two hours later.
During the progress of the scene the light changes from late afternoon sun to dusk.
Victor sits at the dining-room table alone with an empty glass in front of him.
Robin comes in from the garden carrying some orange squash at the bottom of a glass. He is about to go into the dining room when he sees his father. He studies him from a distance, then turns back into the drawing room.
Mary comes in from the hall.

MARY: Have you seen your father?

ROBIN (*he hardly hesitates*): No.

MARY: The Morgans were looking for him to say good-bye. And now the Forsters are going. If you see him ask him to come outside. Tell him the party's nearly over.

ROBIN: Okay.

MARY: And please, for heaven's sake, don't say okay again or I shall scream.

She goes into the garden.
Robin goes back to the point where he can watch his father. Presently he speaks.

ROBIN: Father.

VICTOR: What is it?

ROBIN: They've run out of soda water in the garden. Can I find some?

VICTOR: Of course.

Robin comes into the dining room and opens the sideboard to find the siphon. When he finds it he siphons some soda into his orange squash.

ROBIN: Mother's looking for you.

VICTOR: Yes?

ROBIN: I didn't tell her you were here.

VICTOR: Why? I'm not in hiding.

ROBIN: She said I was to tell you the party's nearly over.

VICTOR: Thank God for that.

ROBIN: Yes. It's not a very good party, is it, as parties go?

VICTOR: No?

ROBIN There's a sort of mood around.

VICTOR: What kind of mood?

ROBIN: Like the last act in *Macbeth*. "Tomorrow and tomorrow and tomorrow."

VICTOR: Couldn't you be a bit more precise?

ROBIN: Everybody seems to be expecting something—something like the wood coming to Dunsinane.

VICTOR: You seem to know *Macbeth* very well.

ROBIN: Yes. I'm acting the Second Murderer at the end of term. But I may be the First Murderer yet because the First Murderer's got mumps.

VICTOR: Tell your mother I'll be out in a minute or two.

70

ROBIN: I needn't say I found you if you'd rather not. Why don't you go to the nursery? Nobody's going to use the tele. The programme's awful today. I'll bring you up a drink and some sandwiches.

VICTOR: I told you I'm not in hiding. And this isn't *Macbeth*. Please go and find your mother, Robin. I want to talk to her alone.

ROBIN: Today everybody wants to talk to everybody alone. Ann's following Mr. Root like a hungry jackal, and Mr. Root's dodging about trying to see Mother like a—

VICTOR: I don't want to know what Mr. Root's like.

ROBIN (*sadly*): I'm the only one nobody wants to be alone with. Not even Ann.

He is going out when Victor calls him back.

VICTOR: Robin. Come here, old chap. (*Robin approaches.*) *I* want to talk to you. (*He doesn't know what to say.*)

ROBIN: Yes?

VICTOR: Do you know a boy at your school called Adams?

ROBIN: Yes. He's got a gold plate in his mouth.

VICTOR: I put it in. Do you know him well?

ROBIN: Oh, pretty well.

VICTOR: Do you know about his family?

ROBIN: Oh, yes, his father ran away with a girl who works in the zoo.

VICTOR: Does he mind much?

ROBIN: Not very much. He said it was more fun in the old days.

VICTOR: Weren't there quarrels?

ROBIN: Oh, that was part of the fun. He said you never knew what was going to happen next. It's very quiet now, he says.

Pause.

VICTOR: Does he see his father?

ROBIN: He goes to a theatre with him every hols and he stays with him for two weeks in the summer. But he feels rather flat about that because the girl from the zoo's never there. She used to look after Pet's Corner and he's passionately interested in pandas.

VICTOR: But he's quite happy—on the whole?

ROBIN: Not at the moment. He had a rat that died.

Pause.

VICTOR: The other day—you know that shop in Oxford Street —I saw a wonderful rat made of plastic.

ROBIN: Oh, good. Did you buy it?

VICTOR: No. Your mother's a bit tired of my jokes.

ROBIN: I'm not. Wouldn't it be grand to have enough money to buy the whole stock? A different catch every day of the week for a year.

VICTOR: I think if I did that your mother would leave me.

ROBIN: Oh well, I expect we'd manage somehow together. Do you mind me saying okay?

VICTOR: I suppose in time I'd get tired of it too. Go and find your mother.

Mary has entered with the Howards during the last of this dialogue.

MARY: Oh, Victor, that's where you've been hiding.

VICTOR: Not hiding.

72

MARY: The Forsters and Morgans went without saying good-bye, and here are William and Margaret. They're leaving too.

MRS. HOWARD: It's been a lovely party. The sun's come out specially for you.

HOWARD: A change after last week. Record rainfall for the month. But of course you missed that.

VICTOR: It rained in Amsterdam too.

MARY: Robin, go and tell Ann her mother's leaving.

ROBIN: Where is she?

MRS. HOWARD: She's by the rockery with Mr. Root.

Robin leaves.

HOWARD: You look all in, Victor. Never known you so quiet.

MARY: He's had a hard day.

HOWARD: Raking in the shekels. Lucky for you people aren't all like me. No trouble with *my* teeth. Every one false.

VICTOR: Then you ought to be careful of the gums.

HOWARD: He's always got an answer, hasn't he?

MARY (*covering for Victor*): There's a new assistant. She's a bit careless. There's nothing more tiring than training a new girl.

MRS. HOWARD: We won't wait for Ann, dear. Tell her we've gone on.

HOWARD: I don't know what she finds to say to that young man.

MRS. HOWARD: I expect much the same as what I said to you. Years ago.

MARY: He's not so young. I'd like to see Ann with someone more her own age. He's too old for her. (*Her anxiety shows a little too much.*)

73

VICTOR (*with just controlled anger*): It's no concern of ours.

MRS. HOWARD (*making peace*): What lovely ear-rings, Mary. I've been admiring them all the evening. Did Victor give them to you?

MARY (*with the slightest hesitation*): Yes.

HOWARD (*to Mrs. Howard*): That's what comes of being a dentist. If I gave you diamonds I'd be suspected of embezzlement.

MRS. HOWARD: If you gave me diamonds nobody would believe it. They'd think I had a lover.

HOWARD: Now we know why you chose Amsterdam, Victor. How did you work the currency, old fox?

VICTOR (*he can stand no more*): I worked no currency. I'm not a black marketeer, William.

He walks from the dining room.
An embarrassed silence.

HOWARD: Well, I am sorry. I never meant . . .

MARY: Nor did he. He's tired and worried, that's all.

HOWARD: I never thought I'd see Victor unable to take a joke. Do you remember a few weeks ago how he had to drink from his own dribbling-glass—

MRS. HOWARD: We aren't always in the mood for jokes, William. Come along, dear, or you won't get any dinner.

HOWARD (*as they move out*): You will tell him, won't you, that I never meant . . .

MARY (*going towards the door with them*): Of course. Don't worry.

MRS. HOWARD: Don't come, Mary. We'll let ourselves out.

They leave.
Mary goes immediately to the dining-room door and calls
"Victor." A pause and she calls again: "Victor."
Clive, followed by Ann, comes from the garden.

CLIVE: He went to the garage.

MARY: Garage?

CLIVE: He said something about going for a drive.

MARY: How odd. He doesn't like driving. He never drives himself if he can help it.

CLIVE: Is something wrong?

MARY: Yes. (*She looks at Ann.*) He had bad news today. A letter from Holland.

CLIVE: I see.

MARY: Are you sure you do?

CLIVE: Yes.

MARY: How can you possibly know what was in the letter?

CLIVE: I can guess. Was he angry?

MARY: Not angry. If you want to know, he wept. I've never seen him weep before.

CLIVE: Ann, you'd better go home.

ANN: Why? I know what you're talking about.

CLIVE: Oh no, you don't. Even Mary doesn't.

MARY: What do you mean?

CLIVE: Christmas was too far off, Mary. I couldn't wait so long. I dictated the letter.

MARY: You . . . ?

CLIVE: I borrowed your room for the purpose. Don't you remember?

MARY: What a bastard you are.

ANN: Don't call him that.

MARY: Oh, go home, Ann. Please.

ANN: Why should I? This concerns me too.

MARY: How can it?

ANN: I happen to love Clive.

MARY: Love? My dear, that's a thing one can sometimes say after bed, but never before.

ANN: How I hate your experience.

MARY: Aren't you looking for it? Go and find it with someone of your own age. Clive's too used for you.

CLIVE: Mary!

MARY (*to Clive*): Aren't you? Even I didn't expect this last clever stroke of yours. An anonymous letter to a husband. He's lived with wives too long, Ann. He's learned too many tricks.

ANN: You drove him to it.

MARY: If you took Clive on, you'd have to learn to love where you don't trust. Better wait a while. You'll be riper for him in a few years, after you've been married, too.

ANN (*to Clive*): She calls you too used. Look at her. Can't you see what she's like now?

CLIVE: I see somebody I love and want, that's all.

MARY: You read too much Zane Grey, Ann. Clive isn't one of your great open spaces. He's more like an over-crowded town. Only I happen to love over-crowded towns. I like a tenement life. I'd be bored with prairies, and the only animal I love has

76

got two backs, not four hooves. Call it "nostalgie de la boue" if you like.

ANN: I call it dirt. I'm free. I want to marry Clive.

MARY: Marriage is not all that clean. (*Ann is crying.*) Do you want a handkerchief?

Robin appears unnoticed from the garden.

ANN: Not one of yours. (*She takes a handkerchief from her bag and accidentally drops a glass object that breaks. Clive is going to stoop for it when she stops him.*) Don't bother. It's only some nonsense her child gave me. (*Robin comes forward and picks up the pieces in silence.*) I'm sorry, Robin. I didn't mean . . . (*Robin doesn't reply, but after gathering up the pieces, makes for the door.*) Give them to me. I can stick them together again.

ROBIN: It doesn't matter. It didn't work anyway.

MARY: Where are you going?

ROBIN: To bed.

MARY: Where's your father?

ROBIN: In the garage.

MARY: Is he still there?

ROBIN: I heard him start the car, but he didn't come out.

Robin leaves the room.
There is a pause. The thought of suicide has come to all three of them, but no one likes to speak first.

CLIVE: I expect he's just fooling about with the engine. Cleaning it or something.

MARY: He never has before.

CLIVE: Would you like me to go and find him?

77

MARY: No, I'll go. (*But she doesn't move either.*) He wouldn't, would he, do anything silly?

CLIVE: Of course he wouldn't.

ANN: What are we standing here for? Somebody's got to go and see.

She starts for the garden. Clive goes after her and takes her arm.

CLIVE: Not you, Ann.

She pulls away from him, then stops in the window, looking at something outside.
Victor enters.
A pause.

VICTOR: Hullo. What is it?

MARY: Where have you been?

VICTOR: In the garage. There are only two places where a man can be alone in his own house.

Another pause.

CLIVE (*to Ann*): I'll see you down the street.

Ann says nothing. They walk to the door.

MARY: I'm sorry, Ann.

ANN: That seems to be the signature tune today.

CLIVE (*at the door*): I shall come back.

Clive and Ann leave.

MARY: You scared us. We half thought . . . Robin heard the engine running.

VICTOR: Yes?

MARY: Of course, I knew you wouldn't do anything silly, really.

VICTOR: Silly is the operative word. I only wanted to be alone, so I sat in the car. Then I remembered something I had read in the papers. I turned the engine on. I shut the garage doors. But the word "silly" came to my mind too, and the headline in the newspaper: "Love Tragedy in West Drayton." This isn't West Drayton, but the district is wrong for tragedy too.

MARY: How could you even have thought . . .

VICTOR: It's unfair, isn't it, that we're only dressed for a domestic comedy. A suicide looks better in a toga, and carbon monoxide poisoning is not exactly a Roman death. I thought of Macbeth.

MARY: Why Macbeth?

VICTOR: "The way to dusty death." Robin hopes to play the First Murderer at the end of term.

Pause.

MARY: What do you want to do, Victor?

VICTOR: If I asked you to give him up, would you do it?

MARY: No.

VICTOR: I understand how you feel. You see, I don't know how to give you up either.

MARY: Somebody has got to do something.

VICTOR: That's what I thought when I went out to the garage. But why should I be the one who acts? There are three of us.

MARY: Clive acted. He wrote that letter.

VICTOR: Clive wrote it?

MARY: I mean he dictated it to the valet.

VICTOR: Then why on earth did he write all that about windmills?

79

MARY: I didn't ask him. I'm sorry, Victor. It was a monstrous thing to do.

VICTOR: I dare say in his place I might have done the same. If I'd thought of it.

MARY: You wouldn't have. You are a good man. Victor, be glad you aren't married to a good woman. The good are horribly hard to leave.

Pause.

VICTOR: Does anybody have to leave? I can forget the letter, Mary. Just give me time. You needn't promise me anything.

MARY: It wouldn't work.

VICTOR: It can. Just don't make things too obvious locally, that's all. You don't hate me, do you?

MARY: Of course I don't hate you. I suppose I love you in my shabby way.

VICTOR: There's nothing shabby about it. It's different, that's all. When the real teeth fail—I'm sorry. Dentistry again.

MARY: One calls the others "false" teeth.

VICTOR: If you go away for a holiday now and then, I won't ask you where.

MARY: There's always somebody who finds out.

VICTOR: That's my problem, not yours. They'll sympathize with you.

MARY: Clive would never agree. He told me that he couldn't bear to go on much longer like this. I asked him to go on till after Christmas, but then he wrote that letter.

VICTOR: If he loves you, he can go on. If I can.

MARY: It's a different love. If it is love. I don't care whether it is or not. I love him any way. It's like a sickness, one of those beastly women's diseases. It probably has a Latin name. (*She is nearly crying and he puts his arms round her.*) I've tried to cure it. Please believe that.

VICTOR: Don't worry, dear. I'll speak to him.

MARY: If I have to choose . . .

VICTOR: I know. You'll choose him.

MARY: I don't know. I don't want to choose. I don't want to leave you and the children, I don't want to leave him. Victor, dear Victor, why can't we sometimes, just once, have our cake and eat it?

VICTOR: I won't take away your cake, Mary. I'll be what they call a complaisant husband.

MARY: Three people have got to be complaisant. It needs a lot of strength.

VICTOR: I can stand it.

MARY: Yes, but can he?

The door opens and Clive comes in. Mary turns abruptly and goes out into the almost dark garden.

CLIVE: Well? This interview had to come, hadn't it? Sooner or later.

VICTOR: Yes. Just stay where you are for a moment. Under the light. Now open your mouth. There's just something—I'm afraid you don't have a very good dentist.

CLIVE: What are you talking about?

VICTOR: That filling in the upper canine—it shows too much. Like an old sardine tin. I would say that it's a very old-fashioned amalgam.

CLIVE (*unconsciously feeling with his finger*): You mean it's a very old stopping?

VICTOR: Better have it done again.

CLIVE: But I can't bear that thing of yours—what d'you call it? The whizzy.

VICTOR: You wouldn't feel a thing. The nerve is probably dead —or I'd use pentothal. Ring up my secretary and make an appointment.

CLIVE: Thanks. Perhaps I will.

VICTOR: We're neither of us young men, Root. The appearance matters. Can I get you another whisky now the party's over?

CLIVE: No thanks. I came back to have a word—

VICTOR: With Mary? She'll be back in a moment. I think she's clearing up the mess in the garden. You know how it is after a party. Why not have another Scotch while you wait?

CLIVE (*hesitating*): It's very kind of you. I haven't been in the mood . . .

Victor pours out two glasses of whisky.

VICTOR: Sit down. (*Clive is about to sit down in the musical chair when Victor stops him.*) Not in that chair. Oh, it doesn't matter. The tune's run out. (*He hands Clive a glass.*) This is good stuff. Black Label. I can only get two bottles a month. I keep it for special friends.

CLIVE: I wouldn't have called myself a special friend.

VICTOR: I think perhaps it would be better if you did. We shall see a great deal of each other from now on, and that is the best explanation, isn't it? Apart from the bookshop. Are dental first editions worth acquiring? Like Zane Greys?

CLIVE: I haven't heard of any.

VICTOR: Speaking as a special friend, I wouldn't see too much of Ann. An impulsive child and too young for you.

CLIVE: Is that—quite—your business?

VICTOR: It worries Mary and anything that touches Mary is my business. It was very good of you, by the way, to give her those ear-rings. She looks beautiful in them.

CLIVE: Yes.

VICTOR: I liked you a lot better when I heard that you'd risked a black-market currency deal to get them for her.

CLIVE: Did she give you any details?

VICTOR: She said something about a currency specialist in Knightsbridge.

CLIVE: She oughtn't to have told you that.

VICTOR: Why? A man and wife don't have many secrets from each other. Except the unimportant ones.

CLIVE: It puts me in your hands.

VICTOR: How?

CLIVE: You could tell the police. I believe I might be put away for two years.

VICTOR: What a strange idea you have of me. It would be a very shabby return for two nice diamonds which I suspect you can't afford. I'm sorry she told the Howards that I had given them to her. She was only trying to protect me. Poor Mary.

CLIVE: Why poor?

VICTOR: You'll know her better in time. Then you'll realize the amount of protection she needs. You and I both have our work. She has no work except the family round. Children, servants, meals—it's not a real vocation. And so to make up she has to have—well, I'd call them illusions.

CLIVE: What illusions?

VICTOR: That she'll love someone for the rest of her life. Physically. In spite of that filling of the upper canine. I'm sorry. That's unfair. I don't suppose my filling would have been any better.

CLIVE: What did you do with the letter?

VICTOR: I tore it up. In time I shall even forget what it said.

CLIVE: I can give you all the evidence for a divorce you want.

VICTOR: I don't want a divorce. The only thing I ask you is to carry on your affair at a distance. You see, there are the children to be considered. May I make a suggestion?

CLIVE: Of course.

VICTOR: Mary's mother is dead. Nobody around here knows that. She can be critically ill three or four times a year. If you require it. She lived in Pontefract, not in Amsterdam. There's a very good Trust House in Pontefract.

CLIVE: Do you really expect us to live like that, not seeing each other except three or four times a year? In Pontefract?

VICTOR: My dear Clive—I'd better get accustomed to calling you Clive—I hope you'll dine with us almost every week.

CLIVE: No. I'm damned if I will. You can be a complaisant husband if you like, I'm not going to be a complaisant lover.

VICTOR: The two are inseparable.

CLIVE: Then I'm walking out. You won't be bothered with me any more.

VICTOR: If you walk out, I think she'll walk out with you.

CLIVE: But that's the best solution for all of us. Can't you see that?

VICTOR: For you and me perhaps. But we've only one object, you and I, to make it a degree less hard for her. I'll make the effort. Can't you do the same?

CLIVE: What makes you think she'd be happier—with the two of us?

VICTOR: The four of us. There's Robin and Sally. She told me herself she doesn't want to choose.

CLIVE: She wants to have her cake and eat it.

VICTOR: That's exactly what she said. Don't you love her enough to try to give her that kind of cake? A child's cake with silver balls and mauve icing and a layer of marzipan.

CLIVE: Bad for the teeth, my nurse used to say.

VICTOR: Not for children's teeth.

CLIVE: You do really love her, don't you?

VICTOR: Yes, I do.

Pause.

CLIVE: Me too. Is Pontefract a bracing climate? (*Robin's voice begins to call:* "Mother, Mother, Mother.") I suppose you can supply me with the dates of the children's holidays and your dental dinners. I'm sorry. I'm trying to work my sourness off on you. I don't want her to feel it.

Mary comes in from the garden.

MARY: Robin's shouting from the bathroom. I suppose he's lost his soap.

VICTOR: I'll go and see.

Victor leaves by the dining room. Neither speaks till he is gone.

MARY: He's talked to you?

CLIVE: Yes.

MARY: What have you decided?

CLIVE: He seems to have done the deciding for me.

MARY: A divorce?

CLIVE: No.

MARY: I suppose that means you are going to leave me.

CLIVE: No. I stay. Under his conditions.

MARY: Thank God.

CLIVE: Are you so pleased?

MARY: Yes.

CLIVE: You certainly must love him.

MARY: I love you, too. Clive, can you blame me if I don't want to lose the past or the future? The past is sixteen years of myself and him, the future is even longer of you.

CLIVE: Longer than sixteen years? I doubt that.

MARY: (*with complete conviction*): It's until death, Clive. (*Clive shakes his head.*) Don't you believe me?

CLIVE: You haven't been to my school. You don't know the lessons I learnt a long time ago.

MARY: What do you know that I don't know?

CLIVE: The future. I'm not being sour, Mary. This is the sad truth, even though I've never loved anyone as much as you. I know that one day I shall get tired of going away at night and leaving you two together. I shall get tired of arranging our holidays to suit his convenience. I shall get tired of all the times when we have to cancel things at the last moment. And I shall get tired of waiting outside the shops in Paris or Brussels while you buy the children's shoes.

Victor comes back into the dining room and, hearing their voices, hesitates.

MARY: And then you'll leave me?

CLIVE: No. Then, when you see how tired I am, you will leave me. That's what I dread.

MARY (*with fear*): I don't believe it's true. I won't believe it's true. (*With confidence and returning gaiety:*) It needn't be true.

Victor comes into the drawing room and joins them. He stands beside his wife. They are a pair. Clive is the odd man out.

VICTOR: If you'd like to stay for dinner, Clive—there are some cold left-overs.

CLIVE: No thank you. I must get back.

VICTOR (*it isn't easy for him to say it*): Come on Thursday. No party. Just the three of us.

MARY: Yes, please come. (*In gratitude to her husband she puts her arm round him.*)

VICTOR: We'll open a bottle of good wine.

MARY: I'll buy it myself at the Army and Navy. What shall I get, Victor?

VICTOR: The Cheval Blanc '53 if he'll come. You will come?

Clive looks at the married pair and sadly accepts his fate.

CLIVE: Oh, yes, I'll come. (*Pause.*) I expect I'll come.

He is turning to go as the curtain falls.